BURNED BY THE
Hawaiian Sun

VINCENT R. PETRUCCI

Inks and Bindings
888-290-5218
www.inksandbindings.com
orders@inksandbindings.com

CONTENTS

This book is dedicated to my beautiful Cousin Mitch and Close friend Michael. Special thanks to Edgar Ruiz for all the sketches and the book cover.

BURNED BY THE HAWAIIAN SUN

Tiziano had just graduated from High School. He was a lusty 18-year-old. He loved adventure and was ready to explore into his next chapter of life. Growing up in a small village in the Sierra Nevada mountains, he really had not experienced a lot beyond his life in Angels. There were the family vacations in and around California. A few trips to the mid-west to visit family and one particular 10-day excursion to Hawaii. It was many years ago, however, Tiziano will never forget. At 18 years old, his family gave him a 7-day graduation present to Hawaii. Tiziano was full of Joy, a dream that had come true.

Tiziano had enjoyed his years in High school, playing sports - baseball, football and wrestling. He was not a Champion yet had competed. He was also involved in other social groups. He had raised sheep and entered them in local fairs. Tiziano was not a straight A student, moreover not a scholar. He was like every other normal 18-year full of testosterone. He had a few girlfriends during High School, nothing but lust.

Tiziano remembers opening up the graduation card from his parents. What a special gift - 7 days in Hawaii and 325 dollars cash. It was 1977. He knew the meaning of money and also had other thoughts in his head.

The flight left 3 days post-graduation. Tiziano had no desire to study and or attend college even though his father was a university graduate and had strongly encouraged Tiziano to attend a least a junior college.

Tiziano was set on travel and intrigued by adventure. He would tell his close friends, I will be a farmer someday, however now I need to find myself. I want to be on my own and go to the Jungles of Hawaii.

It was an early fight from Fresno California to San Francisco on the that hot June day. Tiziano, recovering from the graduation party had never been away from his family for so long. He felt a bit sad, yet was happy he was exploring. His family had some connections in Hawaii and Tiziano had attempted to contact them. One individual stated they would try meet him at the airport in Honolulu. This was on the island of Oahu, The Capital of Hawaii.

Tiziano had taken some medications his mother always gave him when in the car. Tiziano had motion sickness. He was a bit worried and remembers talking to the cute stewardess. She gave him a small bag just in case.

At this time, smoking was allowed on the aircraft. Tiziano did not smoke cigarette, yet did enjoy a nice doobie.

The flight was 5 hours to the Hawaiian Islands. Tiziano was landing in Honolulu. The only thought in his mind was Waikiki Beach. The beautiful Ocean blue skies and lots of girls. Tiziano started to feel nauseated. The flight was a bit rocking. Tiziano remembers the cute tall flight attendant approaching and asking if he was ok. Tiziano looked up yet was not feeling well, air sick.

The next thing Tiziano recalls he was in the back of the fuselage hitting a joint. It was just what Tiziano had dreamed. Hawaii, the land of freedom Paradise, now the nausea had gone. That cute stewardess had done Tiziano right.

Landing in Oahu, Tiziano was a bit uneasy. He had not traveled this long distance alone in the past. The connection was not there. He had called some friends or he thought they were yet nothing. He caught a bus to his hotel that his parents had gifted him for high school graduation. He really did not know much about Hawaii only those 13 years earlier had traveled with his family to an agriculture conference. The hotel was on Kalakaua Avenue in Oahu.

FIRST WEEK ON THE HAWAIIAN ISLANDS

Tiziano alone and already homesick set out. Went down to the beautiful Waikiki scene, the beach. There was Diamond head Crater off to the left of the giant hotel. So many people. The sun was hot. Tiziano was burned in the first hour yet just enjoyed the beach. He had been warned not to stay in that penetrating sun for more than 1 hour. His skin was red and he enjoyed every moment. The trade winds were awesome. All the luxury hotels, bars, night clubs, music, lots of bikinis and the Hare Krishnas are so nice. He went back to the hotel and prepared to go out. Tiziano was burnt that night so flaming red. His parents were correct, however it didn't stop Tiziano. He was on a mission to stay in Hawaii. He had some contacts and wanted to get to Kauai, it was an island near Oahu. The first night out alone went to dinner with drinks. A bit tipsy, Tiziano made his way to the disco. Nice time yet no girls that first night. Home alone. Next morning, he was up early and down to the beach. The waves look so relaxing from the shore, yet once out in the surf the water is powerful. Tiziano wanted to attempt surfing maybe down the road. Each afternoon for the first 4 days, Tiziano attempted to call the contacts his parents had left him. Tiziano alone had No friends on his own. Pay phones

It was 1977 and Tiziano was in pay phone booth for hours trying to make contact with past acquaintance of his family from 13 yrs. ago, no more dimes, finally able to connect with Lelan Nishek. Tiziano knew nothing about Lelan. The card he had stated he had a landscaping and nursey business. Lelan answered the phone. Tiziano even then had a way with words. He explained his situation with Mr. Nishek, yet Lelan stated, "No". He had no work. It was not going to be possible for Tiziano to fly to Kauai, the island Tiziano had researched was around 1 hour by plane, 40 dollars for a ticket. He had the money now, however another few nights in Waikiki it would be gone. Tiziano dimes ran out. He heard nothing but the ring tone.

THREE DAYS TO GO

Tiziano had been in Hawaii for 6 days. He would be flying back home soon. The next day was on the beach getting burned by the hot Hawaiian sun. Tiziano did not care. He loved the water and sun, furthermore wanted to drown his sorrows. What was he going to do? Tiziano continued to dwell on Kauai. He would go to the nearest ABC store in the morning, buy some beer and sit on the beach, enjoying the feeling of the trade winds blowing through his long black and brown bleached hair. By now, his skin was dark. Some of the local would even come by and burn a doobie with him and say, "where you been bra?" as if Tiziano belonged there. Tiziano would not give in. He went back to the hotel on the Waikiki strip and cashed out 5 dollars for change. He made one more attempt to call Lelan Nishek. Tiziano started his campaign again. Lelan said yes.

Tiziano was thrilled. He bought a ticket to Kauai. Tiziano had saved his money and know this would work. The next day he was bound for the airport in Kauai, Lihue airport.

ᴾARADISE ISLAND

Tiziano landed in 1 hour, Lelan was there to pick him up, a tall man, full head of hair with a nice smile, recalls Tiziano. My name Is Tiziano Forli. I was on this island 13 years ago, Tiziano told Mr. Nishek, "My family came on Business and I went along". Lelan acknowledged that, "I recall the name he said". Lelan was a man of few words. Reminded him of his father, a bit younger. "Now an adult, I am back". "Thank you so much for allowing me to work for you". Lelan told Tiziano, he could pay him 1.65 per hour and not promise how many hours a week he could work. "I have no place for you to live as I told you, yet there is a small apartment near Hanamaulu", Lelan said.

Tiziano was taking it all in. The sun was intense however the breeze of the afternoon Tradewinds made it tolerable.

Lelan took Tiziano down to Hanamaulu and paid for 2 weeks rent for Tiziano. Appreciative and excited, Lelan said, "you can use this old Volkswagen van. There are no head lights so do not use at night". "I will take out money from your check to pay the rent", stated Lelan. The apartment was small with a bed kitchen with sink and refrigerator, but no stove. There was an electric 2-burner stove top. Tiziano could make coffee and boil water for pasta. The surrounding outside was vibrant green. Tiziano had researched in his encyclopedia, Kauai has 360 inches of rain each year. Kauai is one of the wettest places on earth. There is an area in the rainforest of Kauai that rains 24 /7. Tiziano smiled to himself and said, "I am here now". Tiziano was content, but a bit homesick. No friends really other than Lelan.

ℜEMNANTS OF THE ℋIPPIES

1977 10 yr. post the hippie movement of America. Tiziano could hear his loving mother say, "Do not interact with those crooks". Tiziano had seen plenty in San Francisco when participating in fairs at the Cow Palace there in daily city. Tiziano was reminiscing and got teary eyed. Now, he was surrounded by them. The rebellious Tiziano decided to cruise around the grassy area. It was like a village with apartments. There were spaces between each apartment which reminded Tiziano of a trailer park, however small spots for dwellings. Hippies were pleasant people. After all, they were just the same as Tiziano, yet they were bit older and it was a movement. They had a vibe. They were a counter culture. Most were middle class white population, yet some Hispanic and black as well. The hippies protested the Vietnam war and felt like they had been alienated from society. Hippies smoked weed. They were mostly about peace and calm. Furthermore, did not like the mainstream materialistic things.

"Hey I am Tiziano. I am from the mainland California". "Ya Bra, you are a Haole". Tiziano was confused. 'Ya bra", the dark long-haired man stated. "I guess, stated Tiziano, "I am just out on the islands tripping". "I am working for Kauai Nursery and Landscaping". "Oh ya, bra" Lelan said to the man. "My name is Elroy. I also work for Lelan". "He is a cool person", said Elroy. Tiziano recalls the curly hair of Elroy. His direct and matter of fact attitude stood out. "Ya bra, mainlanders are called haoles, locals do not like them". Tiziano felt his heart rate increased.

"Don't worry. You work for Lelan". Tiziano took note of what Elroy was saying. He had heard that the local Hawaiians could be rough. "Ya bra, the Mokes". They just smoke the kind and lift weights body surf and chase tourists. Tiziano clarified what is a Mokes. "Bra" Elroy said, "they are the Samoans on the island". "Huge and mean to Haole". "Come on Bra, don't trip". "Try this Kauai electric". Tiziano hit that, "wow feeling great" "You are living around Haoles". "It's a friendly area, Lelan set you up".

Tiziano felt comfortable in the surroundings. Little by little he was becoming part of the scene. The apartment Tiziano lived in was practical. His job was close by. He was meeting people. Lelan had given him a vehicle to use during the day. Tiziano thought about his parents. Yes, he was homesick, however moving forward, he was happy to be there. Tiziano would need to call his family. He knew they would be devastated to know that Tiziano was not coming back to California. This young man … always pushing the.. Envelope.

Kauai Nursery and Landscaping

Tiziano's first day on the job was on the following week. He had been on the island for 2 days and would start soon. Lelan had given Tiziano a map on the directions to the work site. Lelan showed Tiziano the Nursery, the first day he had arrived. 10 days had passed since leaving California.

Tiziano called his parents and told them he would not be back. He was on the island of Kauai and would start working. His mother was very worried and crying on the phone when the line was cut. No more Dimes. Tiziano held back the tears and went to the store to buy some items. At 18 years old, Tiziano was no chef, yet knew how to prepare food. His family had a catering business and small delicatessen. His father had taught him how to cook a few easy dishes - salads and steak. Those were his favorites. Steak was out of the question, not enough money, yet salad was possible.

The first day of work, Tiziano met some of the employees, yet he was nervous. There were all the Filipino's that worked there. There was one time, Tiziano recalls a small man, Francisco. He was old, yet friendly. Tiziano became friends with him. He seemed nice, yet something about him, Tiziano was not comfortable. Francisco offered to pick Tiziano up each day to work, however, Tiziano was driving Lelan's old truck. It appears Francisco acted as the taxi, charging others.

The landscaping and Nursery were huge. There were 3 to 4 crews and about 20 employees. Some were the laborers like Tiziano, planting small plants and or digging trenches for irrigation systems.

Tiziano met another staff member Frankie. He was a Haloe with white skin red hair. He was the supervisor and organized all the projects. Tiziano would work with Louies crew, a long black hair surfer type dude from the hippie time probably. Louie had been in the Vietnam War. Tiziano saw Louie as just a kind individual. He had a nice looking Haole girlfriend. They enjoyed surfing and watching the sun set and had a child together. Louie smoked cool brand cigarettes and always had good weed. A Haole as well, Mexican American. Louie was 10 years older than Tiziano from San Francisco, California. Tiziano liked Louie. He felt comfortable with him. Furthermore, Louie would always give Tiziano advise which seemed to be reliable. Louie had this nice smile and was positive each day Tiziano would come to work. Tiziano knew how to work. Something his father had taught him. Good work ethics. Louie also showed this. He was always busy at work yet enjoying himself as well.

Tiziano was familiar with the irrigation system. He had assisted his father in landscaping his home in California. This was what Tiziano's work consisted of: setting up drip lines on beautiful landscaped properties, Planting palm and Magnolia tree - huge some about 20-foot trees.

The day-to-day work was strenuous and hot. The Hawaiian sun burned and was draining to the body. Tiziano would day dream of completing work and going down to the beach attempting to surf. After all, when in Hawaii, you do as the local's, surf. Tiziano really wanted to learn to ride the waves as the locals would say.

Saturdays and Sundays were off days. Tiziano would hitch hike down to the beach. It was around 15 minutes from Lihue down to coco palms. The old Volkswagen truck was not working that Lelan had loaned. So thumbing was a way of getting around. Riding a bike on the small 2-line roads was dangerous especially for a Haloes. Locals could pick them out from 1 mile away. So far, Tiziano had not had any dilemmas with the locals. He was meeting folks at work and they were nice, yet Tiziano was cautious. Locals were overzealous towards mainlanders. Never stare at them or what they would say why you looking me with stink eyes.

Tiziano recalls a young American couple on the beach one sunny day. They looked as if they were on their honeymoon, playing frisbee. Two Huge locals stepped in and just took the frisbee. I would call them bullies. This was their habit. They wanted to be noticed. Tiziano would just ignore them, yet was aware. Tiziano had many encounters with the locals, being out on the road hitch hiking. Tiziano did not like it, however had no other means of transportation. The locals for the most part had been nice up this time. After all, the entire time on the island of Kauai was an adventure for Tiziano. Surfing was not easy. Tiziano had tried some body surfing. This was new. Tiziano from California and all of its beautiful beaches, yet he lived in the mountains and was not familiar with any type of surfing, but it was scary. The waves were powerful. Tiziano would listen to the young locals whether Filipino, Hawaiians and or a mix. Tiziano learned that Hawaii was really a mix of many different Asian races. There were very few true Polynesian Hawaiians. Some Japanese Chinese, Portuguese Filipino. This seemed to be a melting pot. Various Immigrant groups were in Hawaii. Young Filipino stated to Tiziano, "hit the kind and go for it, bra". "Here at this beach, you can get slammed on the beach". Tiziano did not understand, yet soon found out.

Tiziano did enjoy the warm water of the Pacific Ocean and the salt in the water. Little by little he learned to catch the wave at the top when it started to form and then swim hard and fast and ride the tunnel. Tiziano was a decent swimmer, though not on the swim team. Tiziano preferred football and baseball, traditional American sports yet his family had a swimming pool his entire life. He loved to swim. "Wow this was fun", Tiziano thought, however, he had paid the price many times getting torn apart from powerful waves when he was not able to swim fast enough to avoid the next set. At times, sets would come fast one after another, so you must choose. Tiziano learned when to turnout of the wave and start swimming for the next. Waves twisted and turned your body as if you were a feather. Tiziano would come home after 3 hours totally drained and burnt from the hot Hawaiian sun. Tiziano's hair was long. No longer black yet brown blonde red - bleached from the salt water and sun.

SANTA BARBARA

Tiziano continued work 5 days a week with Lelan at Kauai nursery and landscaping. Weekends were at the beach either Coco Palms or Poipu. There was a great body surfing beach called Brenneckes. The waves were very nice, Tiziano recalls. One particular gorgeous Saturday morning, Tiziano was there at coco palms. The waves were big in the eyes of Tiziano, maybe 3-feet or so. Sitting on the sand, taking in some rays and hitting a doobie. "Hey, how are you?", friendly voice came from behind Tiziano. Tiziano answered, "just enjoying the beach". "My name is Mark". Tiziano explained what he was doing – working and just trippin' post his high school graduation. "I am staying in Princeville. "I am from California", said Mark. "Oh, really?", Tiziano stated. "I live near Fresno, California". Mark appeared nice and pleasant. I live down in Southern California, Santa Barbara. Tiziano was familiar with the place. In fact, his parents had taken their Honeymoon in Santa Barbara.

"What are you doing here in Kauai?", Tiziano asked. "I am on summer vacation". Mark appeared to be around Tiziano's age or maybe little older, around 5'8", light-colored hair and normal built.

"I am in College, yet taking time off". Tiziano was happy he had met another person from California. He was able to relate to him. "Hey would you like to come down to Princeville? I am staying with a few friends", Mark inquired. Tiziano hesitated, "well, I am here getting motivated to ride some waves. I am a neophyte to body surfing. Maybe some other day". At that moment, an older gentleman had come down to the shoreline, "this is my friend Vic. I am staying at his place. I will be out here tomorrow. Let's meet", Mark stated. "We can try some surfing", Mark added.

Tiziano stated he knew nothing about surfing. Mark said he has a surf board and they can learn together.

Tiziano agreed he would try be at coco palm tomorrow and would let them know. The days passed. Tiziano got into some nice waves and was better at body surfing. He would watch the young locals and ask questions. It was all an adventure to this 18-year-old. Learning about the Hawaiian culture and tradition was Tiziano's goal. He was so curious about the island and wanted to be involved in any way possible. Whether it was surfing and or having a local girlfriend.

That next weekend, Mark showed up at coco Palms with his surf board. The older man also showed up. I wasn't quite sure what was going on with Mark and Vic. Tiziano assumed Vic had money. Mark was enjoying that comfort. Tiziano loved girls. He had no desire for a man. They were both pleasant. Mark stated, "Hey, Tiziano, let's travel down the coast". Vic had a car. This was easy, no hitch hiking.

That day, they ended up on some remote beach near Waimea State beach. This is where Waimea Canyon is located. Tiziano had no idea, yet the beach was deserted. It appeared it was uninhabited.

Tiziano loved this. Miles of white sand beaches and no one around at that moment. Tiziano noticed Vic had taken off his swim suit. Mark was there, yet not paying attention to Vic who was laying on the warm sand with the fierce Hawaiian sun on his face. Mark told Tiziano that Vic rented the surf board. "Let's try it", Mark quipped.

Mark braved the ocean. From the beach some 20 meters away, it looked calm and beautiful blue green water. Nice waves were breaking. It did not appear to be beach slammers.

Mark entered the water. "Oh no!", Mark yelled. The coral is near. That part of the beach had lots of sharp corrals. No wonder, Tiziano thought. The beach was empty because it was dangerous.

Let's move down the way, 50 meters north. The water appeared clear, yet the waves would slam against the beach. It was deep maybe 10 meters out, however then the beach and sand was near.

Mark went down hard. I saw the board drifting away from Mark. Tiziano still on the beach, hitting a nice dobbie ran towards the water and swam to retrieve the surf board. Oh my, Tiziano thought, the water looked so nice from the shore, yet, once in the water, it was rough with sets of waves slamming into the beach one after the other.

Tiziano had no concept on surfing. He lay the board and started to paddle out a few meters. About that moment, Tiziano looked up. A powerful wave hit! Tiziano was in the wrong position.

The water threw Tiziano over and over again into coral. The board popped up nearly striking Tiziano in the head. Tiziano's knees were cut by the coral. He was there on the shore, surf board nearby and just shaking his head. The wave had pulled off the ankle tie. The water is so strong, Tiziano thought.

Tiziano felt lucky that nothing else had happened. Mark came over to check on him. "Are you okay? Mark inquired. "Yes, just surfing here is not good. The water was rough. These waves are beach slammers and lots of corals. No wonder it's a deserted island", Tiziano voicing his opinion.

The beach looked so perfect when Tiziano and his friends had arrived that beautiful bright and sunny Saturday morning. Very deceiving, thought Tiziano. Vic walked up. "How is the

Surfing? Mark had a flat affect and said, "Not good". Tiziano did not say much to Vic. He was just there.

Tiziano from that day on stuck to body surfing. He would continue to travel around the beautiful island of Kauai on his days off of work. He would interact with locals and not use the board. Some days, friends would allow him to use their boogie boards which was much easier to ride than trying to stand up on a board. However, Tiziano always knew the locals ruled the beaches. You never really entered the water unless with other locals.

Tiziano had met few friends from work that also loved the beach and body surfing. Therefore, he would travel with them. One of the favorite beaches was Brennecke's Beach in Poipu, located on the south shore of Kauai.

This was a very good body surfing beach. Lots of locals, yet also tourists. The beach was open and no corals. The waves would break off shore so it was very nice to walk out around 50 meters and still the water was not so deep. Tiziano only being 5 feet 6 inches could stand on the bottom of the ocean.

The waves would break out far, therefore, they were not slamming a person to the sand. The waves were easy to catch. Tiziano loved this beach. Waves can really be dangerous, Tiziano thought. Just last week, some mainlander broke his neck from a small wave that broke late. Tiziano had heard the locals' conversations about it.

Tiziano had learned to body surf. It would be nice to have a boogie board yet no budget. Maybe he could buy some Fins, all the locals talked about was the Churchill swim fins.

Tiziano would take some money from his pay check this week. Would ask one of his local friends if he could purchase a pair of Churchill swim Finns. Daniel, a friend of a friend had lots of fins.

These guys surfed each day. This was their lives. "Ronald has a pair, Tiziano", stated Daniel. Tiziano was happy. Bought the pair that were used and fit Tiziano for 3 dollars. Tiziano was in heaven. Now, he was swimming faster and was able to catch more waves. Tiziano was improving each Saturday.

Mark would be coming this next weekend. Tiziano was excited to show him want he had learned. By now, Tiziano's skin was brown and red and his face burnt and nose peeling. The Hawaiian sun was hot.

Tiziano's hair long and multi colored. The sun and salt beached his hair. Tiziano loved the look.

NAPALI COAST

Mark arrived at the coco palms beach the next Saturday. Vic was with him. Vic never said much. Tiziano greeted them both. "I had a great week. I bought a used pair of Churchill Fins. The waves are much easier to catch", explained Tiziano. Vic mentioned to Tiziano that he looked more like a local with the deep tanned skin. "I have been swimming each day", explained Tiziano. One of the guys, Louie, the surfer had given Tiziano a ride to the beach post work and had been surfing every day. Mark explained he also had given up on the surf board and was into body surfing. "Vic bought me some fins", explained Mark.

Wow! They were brand new. It appeared Mark and Vic had some relationship deeper than friends. Tiziano never really got into it, yet he was just along for the adventure. Tiziano knew he was kind and a friend as well. Tiziano was into cute girls. He enjoyed the nice tan skin and long black hair of the Asian girls. Really at this time in Tiziano's life, girls smoking good weed and body surfing was what he craved.

Mark mentioned taking a drive north towards Princeville. Tiziano was a little skeptical, however went along. Tiziano was learning along the way. Mark said that they rented a house. It is so nice. The Napali Coast is nearby. Mark went on to rant and rave about the beauty of the Napali Coast. There is the 2-mile hike along the coast, then 5 mile and then back 10 miles in. Tiziano's eyes became big. Tiziano was working 5 days a week while Mark was with Vic.

"It all sounds great", Mark explained. Tiziano, however is working on Monday. "Today is Saturday. Well, why don't you stay here tonight? We can hike the 2-mile hike tomorrow".

Tiziano thought about the offer on the ride to Princeville on the narrow 2 lane highway. Tiziano had stood out on this road for hours at times hitching rides to go to the beach. This was the same road Tiziano had hitch hiked down going to Hanapepe. Tiziano had met some friends there and went body surfing on a hidden beach a few weeks back.

He recalls meeting this woman one day with Elroy, one of Tiziano's work mates. She was older than Tiziano. It appeared she had lived on the island for some time. Her hair was bleached blonde Skin is brown yet older looking maybe 28 or so. Tiziano thought she's a bit haggard. This was one of Elroy's friends. Elroy, the fat curly haired Portuguese. I never knew why Portuguese was in Hawaii, yet upon talking with others at work, Portuguese grandfather of Elroy had come many years ago searching for work. It appeared to be like many others who had migrated to USA.

Rita was the woman's name - the shark girl. Rita is familiar with this area that was inland from the ocean. Elroy had mention this to Tiziano. It was like a lagoon, beautiful blue clear water that was calm.

In this Lagoon, there were caves so you had to swim under water around 3 meters then surface into these caves. Elroy encouraged Tiziano to explore with Rita. Tiziano felt he could swim under water for 10 to 15 seconds to arrive at the caves. Elroy stated, "You must follow Rita. Stay close and listen to her. The caves were surrounded by sand sharks".

"Oh wow", Tiziano stopped. "No, Tiziano!", stated Elroy. "I am afraid of the sharks". Elroy explained that the shark girl will guide him.

The day was hot there in Hanapepe, small old village. The trade winds were calm. It was early in the day, around 1030 AM. Rita, a woman that did not say much, spoke to Tiziano, "let's go bra", with all her shark teeth around her neck in necklace form. Tiziano was fascinated with sharks, however deathly scared of them. Tiziano was not an accomplished swimmer in the ocean. He always wanted to have a tattoo of a blue shark on his upper arm but Tiziano had no funds.

Tiziano with his snorkel and Churchill fins went for it. He was right behind Rita with so many small beautiful fish. The water was clear and a little cooler than the ocean. This was a lagoon, not sure why Tiziano thought. Fifteen seconds into the dive, a larger fish approached. "Wow! oh no", Tiziano thought. It was the sand shark. Rita motioned back to Tiziano, stayed calm with her hand gestures slowly saying relax.

Tiziano could see the sharks just swimming around, yet really were not near, about 5 meters away. There was sun light. Rita surfaced and Tiziano had already arrived anxious. His heart pounding and still smiling. Rita did not say much, but cracked a half smile as if you made it.

The caves were cool with water dripping. From the upper regions of the caves, small water falls. Ocean water was splashing up on the rocks. The bottom of the ocean swimming in was all sand. No rocks and no corrals at all. It was really heaven. No one around. This is what Tiziano had dreamed about, Hawaii paradise.

Rita had a small pack around her waist, a knife and inside she pulled out a plastic bag. Inside a finely rolled joint and matches completely dry.

Tiziano hit the weed. Feeling a bit anxious, thought I am here thousands of miles away from family and friends. Tiziano enjoyed the moment.

"Let's swim back, Bra", Rita stated. Tiziano at that moment wanted to make a move to kiss Rita who had nice big breasts that were half way out of her small bathing suit, yet thought this was his way back. Tiziano put his selfish thoughts aside, entered the water, cleaned his mask and donned his Fins. The water had become rough, yet once diving down 2 meters, it was calm and quiet. No sharks in site, just 100s of small fish that were all around Tiziano.

Arriving back to the beach area, Elroy was talking with other locals. "Well, how was it, bra?" Elroy asked Tiziano. "This was the best experience", stated Tiziano. Tiziano thanked Elroy.

PRINCEVILLE

They were almost at Princeville when Vic said he would drop Mark and Tiziano off. He said they would meet up later on the 2-mile hike going to the Napali coast. "What is that all about"? Tiziano asked Mark. Vic is strange at times, Tiziano could see that, yet Tiziano did not ask questions and just enjoyed the beautiful time he was having.

Saturday around noon, Mark and Tiziano headed up the hiking path. The rain was on and off and the trail was of rock and slippery moss. Tiziano had on his reef shoes, they were rubber soles and gripped the trail.

Mark mentioned, "have you ever heard of this Napali coast?". "No", Tiziano answered. "Is this where it rains almost each day"? asked Tiziano. "Yes", Mark stated. Here in certain areas, they call it the wettest spot in the earth. It rains nearly 400 inches each year.

The 2-mile hike is nice according to Mark. "I have come here with Vic", he said. It is very beautiful-trees palms and different tropical birds. The rain forest is full of life and we need to be careful. It is dangerous on the path as we get higher up. The cliffs are not forgiving, so do not run even though people are jogging. Tiziano would listen to Mark and take in all the beauty. Tiziano could hear some other hikers coming towards them making their way down the trail.

Tiziano thought, there was the man not much on and his friend a female with a back pack with high laced hiking boots. Nothing else. Heavy bush, huge tanned breasts. Mark signaled yes this is normal on the trail. Tiziano was content.

Mark said, "back to the 10-mile area, was a camp. Everybody partying San Francisco Hippies. Tiziano said he wanted to go. "Today, we cannot", Mark stated.

Another day, they even have helicopters bringing in food and supplies to some rich folks. The path was absolutely gorgeous. Tiziano had no camera. He barely had enough money to survive to pay rent and eat. The ocean and coast line were vast. Heaven on earth, Tiziano thought.

Mark had a pair of binoculars that Vic had loaned him. Tiziano looked down the coast and saw the Dolphins jumping.

More couples walking down. Beautiful Asian girl with her friend. Thongs on their feet, back pack and nude. Tiziano could not help to stop as they walk past, nearly touching them since the trail was not wide. Perfect butt with a black bush. This was motivating. Tiziano wanted to continue trekking to the end of the 2 miles.

Mark explained just around the next climb then we will see the nice beach. It's located in a small cove. Tiziano stopped. He had brought from the canteen some fresh water. He enjoyed the breeze as it hit his sweating face drinking from the canteen.

"There it is, Tiziano", pointed Mark. Wonderful. Fifty meters ahead the beach, plenty of people around. Mark said not to go into the water. The ocean is menacing. Many folks have met their demise here.

Tiziano, one who was a social person, after all, here he was now, thousands of miles from home on some remote beach, started interacting with people. There was some camping with the small tents. Others lying in the sun nude and taking in the strong rays of the Hawaiian Sun. Tiziano by this time 3 weeks on the island was brown. His yellow Bermuda shorts his family had given to him for a graduation present matched his skin.

Mark was sitting up higher on the beach. He saw Vic had showed up. Mark was there talking to him. Vic was nude. Tiziano just was not into Vic. He was talking with others who were offering Tiziano tropical fruits. The day had been a once in lifetime experience for Tiziano, yet not satisfied. He wanted to explore the water. Mark signaled that it's for us to head back. It was near 5 PM. It was Saturday. Mark had invited Tiziano to stay the night, however Tiziano was not into staying. Something said no even though the food and rented house was beautiful.

Mark understood Tiziano and agreed to drive him back to his apartment in Hanamaulu, Kauai. After all, you could drive from one end of the island to other in about an hour.

MITCH

Tiziano continued to work 5 days a week for the Kauai Nursery and land scape company. He was not making any real money, yet was happy he was on his own for the most part. He felt he had accomplished some things, traveling far from home, working, feeding himself and enjoying life at a young age.

Tiziano had been employed 3 weeks. His check each Friday was 109 dollars. His rent was 120 dollars each month and food. It did not leave him with much money. His graduation money was almost consumed.

Louie, his workmate and head of the small crew said that if he works 1 month without being ill, Lelan will increase his pay. Tiziano had good work ethics. He was doing well at work, yet did not like paying the old Filipino, Francisco, for picking him up to go work. However, it was fitting in well with Tiziano's personal needs.

Francisco lived in a community near Lihue, 3 miles from Tiziano's trailer park area. Tiziano had made friends at the small park area, yet wanted to check into renting a room from a family. He had heard about this from friends at work. Francisco stated he knew some folks near his home. They were a Filipino family and had a room to rent at 50 dollars every 2 weeks. There was a shower and kitchen, but the bedroom was small. The area was an add on to the main house and Tiziano would share with 2 others.

Tiziano would go after work and talk with the owner. Francisco said he was very nice. Mr. Almo was his name. He was married, around 35 yrs. old and 2 kids, one boy and one girl who were few years younger than Tiziano.

Mr. Almo said he had a room available. There was an outside entry to the room. The 2 other gentlemen that lived there were older according to Mr. Almo. They are very calm and there should be no issues if he wanted to rent the place at 100 dollars each month, all included.

Tiziano said he would consider it. He explained where he worked and was looking to move. The apartment he had was limited for cooking. This area at Mr. Almo's house had a full kitchen, yet would share it. Tiziano had no reservations.

Tiziano noticed the neighborhood seemed quiet. Families are mostly Filipinos. Tiziano would chat with Lelan and explain what he wanted to do.

The next week would be Tiziano's last week at the small cottages near Kauai surf resort.

Tiziano had 2 suit cases. Nothing much. His Churchill Fins. The move was easy as it appears this will be a good change. Mr. Almo stated he could use their phone to call the main land and speak to Tiziano's parents.

This was a big relief. Each and every time to call to Angels would take going to a pay phone. It was a hassle. The move to Mr. Almo's house was all positive for Tiziano. Lelan also thought it was wise move as it is safe and saving few dollars.

The following weekend Tiziano moved in. His room was quiet. He met the 2 other gentlemen. Both 20 years older than Tiziano. Chip was a Filipino man, dark skin and dark black full head of hair. His eyes were a bit red and he looked worn in the face, yet had a smile. His breath smells of liquor. No big deal, thought Tiziano.

Mr. Almo assured Tiziano that the roommates were honest and would not bother any of Tiziano's items. The other gentleman was older than Chip and Tiziano never saw him much. He had rented the room yet stayed on the south shore with his family according to Mr. Almo.

Tiziano now lived near Francisco. He no longer paid for the car ride, however continued to go back and forth to work with Francisco. They went from Hanamaulu straight to the work site.

Tiziano's work at KNL was moving along. He learned more about planting huge magnolia trees, palm trees and other tropical plants. Some of the trees were over 20 feet tall. The trees came from Kauai nursery and landscaping, then replanted at site's hotels, homes and golf courses.

Tiziano was able to enjoy the beautiful landscape of the island and getting paid. It was near the weekend and Tiziano had been thinking about his cousin Mitch. He lived in California and was in the Navy. Mitch was a friend and cousin. Tiziano had spent time with his cousin growing up and they were close even though they lived in different towns. Mitch lived near the coast which is some 2 hours west of Tiziano. Mitch was an outgoing individual who did not like attending school.

They would spend time together during holidays and or in the summer. His cousin similar to Tiziano also have an affiliation for adventure. They were both mischievous. At the time, Mitch had not completed high school and was a member of the United States Navy. Tiziano called Mitch one Saturday from the Mr. Almo's phone and he was able to make contact. Tiziano wanted his cousin to experience this beautiful island. They could have so much fun together, however at this time, his cousin was not available to come to Kauai.

Mitch appeared somewhat distraught. Things are not going so great in the US Navy. "I am going to leave", he said. Tiziano was sad to hear this, but he wanted the best for his cousin.

A few days later, Tiziano received a call from Mr. Almo. His room was only a closed door away down 3 steps. "Someone is on the phone for you, Tiziano", he continued.

His cousin's voice sounded great. Tiziano was content to hear that Mitch would be arriving in Hawaii. Tiziano knew nothing and did not ask questions. He only knew that his friend and cousin would be there with him.

$\mathcal{A}$RRIVAL

Mitch called from the Lihue airport and said, "I am here". "Wow!" Tiziano thought. "How can this be true"? Is this a dream? Upon arrival to the airport, accompanied by Tiziano's friends, he saw his cousin's smile. Long golden hair, tank top on and nothing else.

"Where are your things"? Tiziano asked. I have my tooth brush and nothing else. No suit case, nothing.

Mitch explained, "I hitch hiked from Moss landing to San Francisco". "I caught the flight and I am here", he continued. "Come, lets go to my place", stated Tiziano. "I want to familiarize you with my friends and the home", he furthered.

Mitch had left the US Navy. He had told his parents he was joining his cousin in Hawaii and left.

Each day Tiziano continued to work. Mitch was down at the beach body surfing. Mitch had grown up on the coast of California. He was familiar with the ocean. Tiziano gave him his Churchill Fins to use for body surfing.

During the weekend, they were both at the beach, body surfing looking for girls and having the time of their lives. Mitch was the type all girls were attracted to. His body was lean, brown skin and muscles head to toe. There were some days Mitch was gone. He was staying with girls.

Tiziano was a bit jealous, yet kept working. After all, when Mitch did not come back home, he always had cash. He assisted in paying rent and there was beer, food and weed.

Tiziano could not complain. Some nights Mitch would show up with 2 tourist girls. He had been down at the resort and scored. Tiziano was also enjoying the time. "This is my cousin Tiziano", Mitch would introduce me to his girls. We would all party either at the resort around the pool and or at the beach with a camp fire. It was really remarkable. Easy for Mitch to have girls around. Lots of girls.

Tiziano was not in the same category when it comes to attracting girls. Mitch was like Elvis. When out on the road hitch hiking, there was no more waiting. Mitch would take his shirt off. Cars would stop immediately and at times 2 cars. It's different now. There's always money, good weed, food at home and girls.

BACK TO NAPALI

Tiziano's cousin was spending less time at home. Mitch was a social person and there are always people around him. Not sure what he was doing, yet I knew he was not working and always had money. He had new shorts while Tiziano was still wearing his favorite yellow shorts his parents gave to home for High School Graduation.

The next Saturday, Mitch showed up early. "Hey!" he stated, "let's go to the Napali coast". Tiziano had been there with Mark, yet Mark had not been around since his cousin came to the island.

Tiziano stated, "oh, so you know about the Napali Coast"? "Yes, I heard it's awesome", explained Mitch. "Yes", Tiziano stated, "I did the 2-mile hike with a friend I met Mark". "He is from California as well".

Mitch had met a younger friend and his father. They had been body surfing and spending time together. They are treating me like family. I can order whatever I want. Two breakfasts in the morning. Mahi Mahi for lunch and dinner. Tiziano was like "I told you so". "Mitch is like a movie star". People are attached to him, men and women alike. They wanted to be around him once they knew him.

Mitch was going on and on. Tiziano took it all in. "Let's do it!", Mitch said. "So, what about work?", Mitch asked. "I will be back on Monday", Tiziano answered. The older man and his son along with Tiziano and Mitch headed north for the Napali coast in the rented car. "I am interested in the 6- mile hike", stated Mitch's friend. Tiziano did not recall his name, yet it felt as if they saw Mitch as God himself.

The day was hot with occasional rain. Not many hikers on the trail. The sky so blue with the beautiful Pacific Ocean and the breaking waves in the distance.

So much Vegetation on the trail. The clean fresh air, smell of orchids and bird of Paradise plants. The Napali coast was another example in Tiziano's eyes. Heaven on Earth, very pleasant.

The hike took 3 hours. Tiziano was jogging some of the trek. Tiziano was anxious to see how different the 6-mile hike area was compared to the 2-mile hike Tiziano had taken with Mark.

Lots of tourists. Many campers and so many nude people. "Wow!" Tiziano thought the beach was accessible. Tiziano did read one sign "ENTER THE OCEAN AT YOUR OWN RISK ROUGH UNDER TOE"

Tiziano used precaution, yet did enter the water. So clear, so warm. Mitch came down. "Sorry", he explained, "I was assisting my friends". "No problem", responded Tiziano. "I am enjoying myself. I had always wanted to explore this".

The day went on. Tiziano started talking with a couple of girls. They were from Chicago, Della and Rose. Not bad, Tiziano thought. Della was short, but with long black hair, beautiful skin, maybe Hispanic and or Italian descent. Rose was bit taller with long straight black hair. She has a small mouth and tiny eyes. Both were very out spoken. They like to hit the joint and stated they were on vacation for 2 months before going back to start university there in Chicago. "Nice", Tiziano thought and said, "just like me", yet Tiziano had no desire to go to any college and or University.

He would go back home some day and work on his family's farm.

Tiziano shared where he was from in California. "I am living up in Hanamaulu. Working just finding myself trippin' this summer. My parents gave me one week for a graduation present, yet I knew 7 days was not enough. I left Oahu and flew here. I am just lucky, I guess".

"Landed this job. Have a place to live and now my cousin is here". Della had this nice smile. First impression, she likes Tiziano. This was the first girl that he felt liked him since arriving. Sure, there were the ones that his cousin had brought over, however they were just following Mitch's wishes. If you are with me, you are with my cousin as well. It was not bad, yet this was better. Tiziano introduced Della and Rose to Mitch.

ℱRIENDS

The next day, Tiziano woke up at the resort on the lawn chairs near the pool side. He had a few too many adult beverages and was a bit dizzy that morning, but had a smile on his face. Mitch was in the room of the Rose and Della.

Tiziano had a great time, enjoyed Della, however at 2 am went for a swim and feel asleep. The morning sun in his eyes woke him up.

Tiziano had met new friends, yet they were going back to Oahu. Tiziano contemplated the situation. Mitch had made his mind. He wanted to travel with the girls and explore Honolulu.

Tiziano had now been working 6 weeks at KNL. He enjoyed his job; however, the new friends were sweet. Tiziano had lust for Della.

The days went by and Tiziano spent each day down at the resort with Della and Rosa. Mitch would come and go. He was enjoying his friends near Princeville.

Tiziano explained he wanted to join them in Oahu, yet would work two more weeks. Make some money then fly over. He knew it was a chance he needed to take. Money was short. He was not his cousin Mitch. It seems Mitch had all he needed without working. A lucky young man. Great people skills.

Tiziano thought that Della could find another guy. Tiziano was satisfied with his decision. His libido was extremely strong, however would control it for now. Each day he thought about his new friend Della. When together they would go to the beach and hang out. Tiziano loved to kiss. Della always complimented Tiziano. "You are very good at kissing", she would say. This just made things worse. Tiziano would stick to his plan. Even though he enjoyed each day, still he would work a few weeks.

ALONE AGAIN

Monday morning, Tiziano would say bye. He was off to work. Mitch, Rose and Della were off to Oahu. Tiziano encouraged Della to call Mr. Almo's house when they found a place. Rose had a friend in Waikiki beach. It sounded as if they had an apartment.

Tiziano was sad, however the next day, a call came in. One of Tiziano's friends from California, Mickey. He had played baseball with Tiziano. Mickey was an outstanding player and had been drafted by a professional team.

"Hey Tiziano, my mother spoke to your mom last week at the grocery store", he said. They mentioned you were in Kauai". I am off to New York to start my professional baseball career, yet I have 2 weeks and would like to fly out", explained Mickey.

"Sounds great!", Tiziano replied. "I am working, but on the weekend, I have some time", he furthered. Mickey was a tall and strong young man. Could throw a fast ball 90 miles an hour. Tiziano himself was a Pitcher in baseball yet not near the quality of Mickey.

Mitch called after several days and stated he was on Oahu. We are staying in some studio apartments here on Waikiki beach. The lollipop night club is below our place.

The apartment is small. "We will see you soon, Tiziano" he said then hung up. I could tell from his voice it was not stop there for him. Mitch was going full throttle party mode. He stated was at Waikiki beach each morning and had met a young lady. Her father renting her an apartment.

Now Mitch was living with her and only going to the studio apartment one once a week. Tiziano knew Mitch was in heaven with girls, money and food. He's not working. Mitch was like a star. He always had people around him -families, girls and men. They all liked him. They all contributed.

Mickey arrived at the Lihue airport. It was crazy to see him. Mickey was a man of few words. He always had a smirk on his face, a smile. Very nice and awesome athlete. He had won many competitions in High school. Always number 1 in baseball and football. "Let's get something to drink ", Mickey said. Tiziano took him down to his place in Hanamaulu. "Here in Hawaii, they drink the local beer primo", I said. At 18 years old, Tiziano liked to drink beer, yet never saw anyone drink as much as Mickey and never be intoxicated.

Tiziano was anxious to show Mickey what his new past time was on the island. No longer baseball every day, but body surfing.

Mickey was quick to learning fact was Tiziano could not get Mickey back from the ocean. During the week, Tiziano was working. Mickey was at coco palms and or hitch hiking out to Poipu beach.

Brennecke's Beach was the best spot. Tiziano had been there several times. Mickey loved the place. Tiziano would leave for work at 7 am and Mickey would also leave for the Poipu. Tiziano finished work at 4 pm and Mickey would be home until 7pm. Mickey was dark tanned by now.

Did not say much, however, Tiziano knew he was enjoying himself. "Let's go out tonight, Tiziano", he said. "Yes, down to the resort Kauai surf and of coco palms", I answered.

The issues were get cleaned up and go hitch hike. Tiziano had no car, no motorcycle, and bikes on those narrow roads were not safe at all especially being a haole. Tiziano explained this to Mickey.

Mickey was like, "do not worry, Tiziano. You are with me". Yet, Tiziano tried to explain to Mickey that the local Samoans are rough. "They call us Haoles. I have observed them beat down mainlanders".

Mickey did not say anything. "Let's go!", Mickey said finishing a primo. Mickey was not like Mitch when it came to car stopping, however, it only took 20 minutes that evening around 8 pm. Arriving down at Kauai surf.

The resort was full. The trades blowing. The evening's so perfect. They were having a luau. The resort would have them down at the beach fire pits and plenty of food so guests of the hotel could partake in a real Hawaiian Luau.

The serving table was awesome. Extremely beautiful. All the flowers and fruit. The cooked pork. Kauai nicked name the Garden Isle. It was really living up to its name on this night with the Polynesian Dancers and the smell of the fresh orchids.

Lots of tourists. Tiziano himself was a tourist, yet after 6 weeks on the island, he felt like a local. Mickey appeared to be having fun.

Tiziano told Mickey just fall in line. "We are part of the guests. Take a plate and enjoy" Tiziano said. "Continues to have fun and explore. So much food goes to waste so help yourself".

Tiziano had a few adult beverages yet really did not consume many. He wanted to function the next day, however Mickey was nonstop. Dancing with a sweet tourist's young lady, which he ended staying with all night.

Tiziano stated he would be out around the pool. Tiziano would talk with some locals enjoying some good Kauai electric.

The next morning, Tiziano woke up at the pool area. He had stayed the night again sleeping on the pool furniture. Not the best practice, yet he did not want to travel back hitch hiking last night since it's too dangerous.

Mickey made it back to Hanamaula the next morning. "How was it?", inquired Tiziano. "So good. Young lady was from New York. We had a fantastic time", he answered. Let's go body surfing in Poipu, Tiziano", Mickey stated. Saturday morning. Such a crisp day. Great idea, thought Tiziano.

Tiziano and Mickey made it out to the main road. Highway only one from north to south on Kauai. A car picked them up immediately. Thirty-five-minute ride and they arrived at Poipu beach. The best body surfing beach around Brennecke's Beach.

The sun was already warm at 9 am. No one around the tourists were still hung over from the night before. The locals would show up when the hot and sexy tourists were on the sand.

Tiziano placed a small towel on the beach. Mickey had a few primos in a sack. Before Tiziano could say a word, Mickey had already swum out. "My god!" Tiziano remarked. He was out 100 meters out from the shore. The waves were nice that day. A small storm had pushed in causing the waves to be a bigger, maybe 3 feet, however, breaking very nice off the beach front preventing any beach slammers.

This was the beauty of Brennecke's Beach. The waves broke out 100 meters from shore preventing getting slammed or badly injured.

Wow! the feeling of riding the powerful wave through the tube or tunnel as wave formed and then rolled out down the beach. Tiziano had been body slammed many times hitting the sand. Board surfing getting cut from coral on a beach that they should not have been on. This was a special beach.

Tiziano hit that nice doobie, walked out and put on his Churchill Fins. The water so warm heavy salt. Tiziano's skin was dark brown. His face red brown and peeling skin from too much Hawaiian sun. It was burned.

Tiziano knew Mickey would not come in for hours. Mickey was addicted to the waves. Tiziano also enjoyed them, yet not to the extent that Mickey was into them for.

ᴅARK

Tiziano was doing well that bright crisp Saturday morning. He saw a few younger locals come near him riding the waves. The next thing Tiziano felt was a powerful blow to the face. He touched his nose and blood running down. His front tooth loose with lots of pain.

"Get the fuck off the beach, haole". "You are on my beach". Tiziano looked up. It was a young local boy, about 13 yr. old or so. Tiziano out of frustration grabbed the adolescent and said, "why the fuck you doing this?"

The young dark adolescent yelled at Tiziano, "you are not getting off this island alive, Haole!" Tiziano was in shock. He knew about the stories of messing with locals. He knew the consequences that Elroy had stated to him. Mokes were nothing to deal with. Elroy always said stay away from them. They are mean and will destroy you.

Tiziano swam back to the beach. He lay there in the sand for a few minutes then tried to signal to Mickey. "Come back. Let's go!" This beautiful day at the Brennecke's Beach was over. So many things racing through Tiziano's head.

Mickey waved Tiziano off. Mickey was not coming in. Tiziano swam out to Mickey. Tiziano explained to Mickey what happened.

Mickey looked at Tiziano with his half smile and smirk face. "Don't worry, Tiziano, it will be alright". Tiziano went on and on yet Mickey was not hearing it.

Tiziano rode a few more waves. He made it back to the shore. Tiziano laid down in the sand, yet he was not comfortable. He was scared and anxious. He knew the locals were not going to take this well.

Tiziano looked up to his left. There they were 2 big Mokes and the young Hawaiian local kid. He saw him point to Tiziano. At that moment, Tiziano needed to either stand his ground and or avoid the confrontation.

Tiziano started to make his way towards the road through the jungles of the surrounding of Poipu Beach. He was walking fast trying to signal to Mickey. He could see Mickey saw all the commotion.

Tiziano waving his arms, "come on, Mickey, there is trouble". "Let's leave, hurry!", Tiziano was yelling now and started to run. The Mokes were not far behind. Mickey made up to the road with Tiziano.

"I told you, Mickey", Tiziano stated. Mickey, a person of few words did not say much. They were at the intersection. Tiziano put his thumb out and a car stopped. "Let's go"!

The young male tourist asked, "where you going?". "North, towards Lihue", Tiziano was trippin'. My god we just made it out of there.

Mickey stated those people had a gun. I never thought this would happen. Tiziano knew that the stories Elroy told him were true. This was not the first encounter Tiziano had with locals, however, this was the worst.

The young male tourist was really not paying attention to Mickey and Tiziano. Tiziano was still recovering from running for his life from the locals. They must of ran over 1 mile before they were picked up.

His heart rate was elevated, anxious and scared. Mickey appeared to be disappointed that he was not able to body surf anymore that day. Tiziano looked up and saw the driver they had hitched a ride with appeared stoned. His eyes were closing. Tiziano motioned to the young driver who had identified himself as a Stewart on united airlines. "Hey! watch the road", exclaimed Tiziano.

The driver looked at Tiziano then in the next second, the car started to drift to the right. TIziano again yelled, "watch out!" The car was out of control. The intoxicated driver was lost. It was raining hard. The slippery road put the car in a spin, once coming into contact with the wet grass on the side of the road near the sugar cane fields, it was over.

The car flipped over and over again. The intense impact caused Tiziano to hit his head on the front wind shield glass cutting his head. Blood was all over. The car came to a stop in the middle of the 2-lane road. Traffic backed up. Mickey in the back seat was alert and no issues.

Mickey signaled over to Tiziano, "what happened?" "This fool just almost killed us", Tiziano answered. Two near death experiences in less than 1 hour. Mickey stated, "your head has a cut". Tiziano looked in the mirror, nothing but a small cut, abrasion. Tiziano said, "looks worse than it is".

Soon the police arrived. Tiziano explained what had happened. He told the police from the local station locals were after them and that they were running for their lives. Then made it to the road and were picked up by this individual.

The Stewart was being looked at by the ambulance and EMT. Tiziano along with Mickey were taken back to the rented room in Hanamaulu Kauai by the local police officers.

You young men are lucky nothing serious really happened. Tiziano was asked by the police officer if he wanted to see a doctor, but Tiziano said no.

Waikiki

Mickeys time on Kauai had come to an end. He was back to California and then off to New York to start his professional baseball career. Mickey had enjoyed his time. Tiziano could see it.

His tall tanned body and smiling face proved to Tiziano that Mickey had a few weeks that he could remember for a lifetime. Two days later, Tiziano escorted Mickey to Lihue Airport in Kauai. Tiziano felt a bit homesick.

He had an idea he wanted to maybe go back home after all the crazy things that had happened. He really did not want to call his family. He thought this would just cause Tiziano to feel sad.

Mr. Almo stated your cousin had called the other day. Tiziano was excited. The next morning before work, Tiziano would call Mitch.

Tiziano needed to make a decision. He was here alone again. It had been 2 months on the island. He had met some of the goals he wanted to achieve. His body was dark tanned. His hair so long and bleached brown red orange. Tiziano liked the look. He had met a girl. They had slept together. His body surfing skills were better and was able to know some locals.

Tiziano was concerned of the locals from Poipu beach. The island was small. He had reservations about going out at night. Perhaps these locals were searching for him. Would they recognize Tiziano?

Mitch picked up. "Hey bra, are you coming to Waikiki"? "It is crazy here, Tiziano", mitch stated. I am living with a nice sexy girl. Tiziano answered, "Oh! how is it"? "Things are going well, yet have not seen D and or Rose", said Mitch.

"I go by sometimes", explained Mitch. Tiziano told Mitch that he was planning on discontinuing his job at Kauai Nursery. "I am going to leave next week", Tiziano said. Mitch was excited.

Tiziano wanted to see D and Rose. He was craving intimacy. Mitch had the address and Tiziano was going to move there.

The next day at work, Tiziano gave his notice to Lelan. He thanked him and was so happy for Lelan Nishek. All the wonderful things Lelan had done for Tiziano. Working at Kauai Nursery and landscaping. It had been Tiziano's real first job. He made 109 dollars each week. I .69 per hour. Tiziano smiled and left back for Hanamaulu.

Tiziano thought, "I am a young man, on graduation vacation from High school, yet did not want to go home". Was down to the last day of a wonderful time on Oahu Hawaii, Lelan had taken Tiziano in. Lelan had saved Tiziano. He could not appreciate him enough, yet Tiziano needed to go.

Tiziano was the kind of person that seemed not to be content.

Tiziano did have to worry about the locals from Poipu, yet that was not why he wanted to leave. He just was board of work and lonely. He wanted to see his cousin and meet with D, his girlfriend from the Napali Coast. It was Time to go. It was a vacation. The job at KNL assisted Tiziano with his goals to learn about the cultures of Hawaii. It was the next phase now.

KALAKAUA

Tiziano arrived on Oahu. He took a bus from the airport down to Kalakaua Avenue. He made his way over to the lollipop. "Wow!", Tiziano thought. This is a topless lounge. The apartment complex was just above.

Mitch had mentioned to Tiziano to just look for the flashing lights, then look up. The small apartment complex was right above the lollipop. Tiziano was greeted by his cousin Mitch and his new gf, a petite sandy blonde-haired girl. She had a dark tan. Tiziano recalls her finger nails long were perfect with red polish, and matching the toenails. "This is Cherry", stated Mitch. "Pleased to meet you", Tiziano stated. Cherry did not say much. She did not need to with that shape of a body large breast and a sweet smile.

"Let's go up to the apartment", Tiziano told Mitch. "Go ahead, Tiziano. D and Rose are not talking to Me", Mitch said. "Why?", Tiziano asked. "Well, I guess because of Cherry", Mitched reasoned.

Tiziano knocked on the apartment door 325, the third floor. The complex had maybe 30 apartments. Lots of action in the area. The loll pop down stairs, then out the window of the small studio apartment was Kalakaua Avenue.

People coming and going. The ABC convenient store. All of the needs were in close proximity of the apartment. The Hare Krishna was chatting on the street light candles and asking for money. You saw groups of tourists who appeared to be from all over the world.

D was happy to see Tiziano. "I am working at the pizza parlor on the corner", D stated, "and Rose is a waitress", she added. "We are having a great time, yet Mitch does not come around. He is with Cherry". Tiziano was okay with that. The apartment was tiny, yet had bathroom kitchen. One bed and couch. Tiziano would sleep on the floor with a thin mate. D was not as liberal with her body as she was in Kauai. Maybe she had another boyfriend. Tiziano would take it day by day .

Tiziano was to meet Mitch down at the beach. It was 100 meters around the corner. There it was, Waikiki beach with so many people and beautiful girls all over. The first week Tiziano had been in Hawaii nearly 9 weeks ago. Tiziano can remember the first day, burnt by that Hawaiian Sun. Now, Tiziano's brown skin with his long brownish hair and a puka shells around his neck.

Mark had given the Puka shells to Tiziano. "These will keep you safe and bring you good luck", Mark told Tiziano. Some Hawaiian myth. Tiziano needed all the luck he could get. The last few weeks had been difficult. Two times nearly killed. The vacation was turning a bit dark, however, Tiziano was positive and felt being back on Oahu would be smooth.

Tiziano saw Cherry and Mitch was laying on the beach on a beautiful towel. It seemed all the nice gifts Cherry had bought. Mitch had mentioned Cherry s father had rented her the apartment.

Cherry was like Tiziano, just on vacation, on daddy's budget. Tiziano's budget from his parents had run dry weeks ago. Tiziano had been on his own now for the last 8 weeks working at Kauai Nursery. His family's gift was for 1 week on Oahu and then back to the mainland. Tiziano had proven them wrong, yet his goal was not to prove them wrong. He was out for adventure. His love for Hawaii had started on that family vacation back in 1967 when Tiziano was only 5 yrs. old.

Tiziano has craved Hawaii ever since.

Mitch was with Cherry. She bought him whatever he wanted for breakfast in the morning, new shorts and sun tan lotion. Tiziano had his old yellow shorts, his reef shoes he used all the time even to go out at night, his 2 church hill fins and his Hawaiian slings for spear fishing.

"Hey! Let's rent the boat, Tiziano", Mitch pointing over to the rentals. We can go out to blue water where the reef ended, spear some fish bring them back here to sell". Tiziano was game. Mitch had new fins. Cherry had bought him a new mask and snorkel. Getting out to the blue water was no easy task.

The waves were breaking in on the shore of Waikiki. You just need to navigate them. The plastic 6-foot boat could fill with water easily. Mitch had some experience with sailing. His father was a sailor and they had 2 small dory sail boats back on the mainland of California.

Mitch had grown up in small fishing village on the California coast. Tiziano had grown up in the mountains. He knew about animals, a bit farming skill and nothing about the waves and ocean.

Now 9 weeks on the islands, he had become educated about the strength of the ocean and respecting it…

The depth water near the shore of Waikiki was around 4 or 5 feet. There were some small waves yet mostly flat. Once you got past the break of the waves, it was smooth ocean. Lots of boats passed the reef. Cruise line ship's full of tourists. This is where Mitch wanted to go, just to the edge.

Tiziano and Mitch had been diving back in Kauai. Tiziano bought the Hawaiian slings with his last pay check, yet had not found any nice spots to dive. This was all new to Tiziano and his cousin. It was not difficult, yet always the thought of the big fish coming into the picture. Tiziano had seen some sharks under water when swimming with Rita in the caves back on Kauai. He was anxious about them. They say blood in the water can attract sharks. Sharks can smell the blood from other fish from a far distance. Elroy mentioned that to Tiziano. A small amount of blood can be detected by a shark 100 meters or more away.

The ocean for spear fishing was dangerous. The water was powerful with rocks and coral nearby. Tiziano was accurate. He was able to connect with the fish easily. Mitch was a natural. The spear was around 6 foot long, thin and with a thick rubber band. Cocking the spear was easy. Sliding your hand through the rubber band and down lower part on the spear, then lease. It was powerful and deadly.

As Mitch maneuvered the small boat out towards the deeper blue water, Tiziano just took in all the beautiful landscape of the Waikiki

Bay, moving out towards the cruise ships and watching all the tourist give surfing a try. Diamond head just off to the south, the volcanic crater. It only had erupted one time, about 1000 years ago. It was truly gorgeous. The smell of the water. The beautiful Hibiscus plants out lining all of the huge hotels overlooking Waikiki.

"Hold on to the Fins and the masks spears. This wave I did not catch at the right time", stated Mitch. The boat went up high on the pinnacle of the wave with lots of white water splashing down, a near miss of the boat being completely submerged.

Made it. The ocean was now calm out near the end of the reef of Waikiki Bay. It was quiet. Tiziano could not hear any people talking and or laughing, yet just the sound of the spray and breaking of the waves towards the shoreline.

Mitch was quick to dive in. The water here was near 3 meters deep, yet if you went 2 meters towards the blue water it dropped off fast. "Wow! Amazing!", Tiziano thought.

"Scary", Tiziano could only think of one thing- Sharks. We were out in their ocean; we were looking for fish that sharks consumed. Mitch had already speared 2 fish. Nice size beautiful colors. Tiziano had learned some of the names of the fish. Saddle wrasse was the most abundant fish that lived around the reefs. Tiziano really did not care about the name. The goal was to catch the fish then sell on the beach.

Mitch had pointed out that there were the sea snakes. Tiziano knew nothing about a sea snake. One bite from the venomous snake could cause death. The snake was not aggressive, yet if it was surprised it might bite.

The snake blended in with the sand at the bottom of the ocean floor. Tiziano was not near the bottom. Tiziano could hold his breath for a few seconds. He had always practiced at his parents swimming pool back home. "I see that small fish", Tiziano started to get the hang of it. The issues were the fish looked much bigger in the water than outside.

Tiziano looked in the boat over 20 fish. The boats floor was bloody with fish. The morning turned to noon. The Hawaiian sun was hot.

Tiziano had no hat, just the yellow Bermuda shorts that he had received as a graduation gift some 10 weeks ago. Tiziano loved the shorts. Bleached from the sun and salt water, they were perfect.

Tiziano was ready to go back to the beach front. The afternoon trade winds had started. Mitch came back to the small dory. "Let's head back" Tiziano said as he attempted to paddle the boat. It was difficult to steer. The boat was heavy with fish. Three people in the boat and 25 fish. Winds were strong. Mitch jumped out of the boat and swam to the front. He started pulling the boat and attempting to get back into the area where the waves where breaking. The current would assist with paddling. Tiziano was amazed how his cousin just took charge. Finally, after 30 minutes of paddling and struggling to get the small boat back tom the Waikiki shore, they were on track.

Tiziano was exhausted.

The waves were at 4 feet with strong breaks and the wind blowing. Mitch had nearly capsized the boat. Mitch had saved the small crew with the fish. Mitch's girlfriend was there. She had taken off her bikini top enjoying the ride. It as if she had no care in the world. That is my brave Boyfriend. Tiziano praised his cousin.

Back at the shore people were starting to leave the beach. The evening had set in.

Tiziano had purchased small ice chest and made a sign. ***Fresh Fish For Sale***. Many locals would walk up and make mean comments. You mainlanders, go back home!

Tiziano along with cousin stayed until the last fish had sold. The sun was down.

Tiziano was burned by windy sunny all day. Tiziano's skin was dark brown and his cousin had an awesome tan.

Many locals considered Tiziano as if he was a local himself, with the long brown reddish hair and deep tanned body. "Fifteen dollars", Tiziano stated to his cousin. Mitch appeared frustrated.

The idea had not really worked out, yet his girlfriend had rented the boat, so all the money was profit. The 3 of them made their way to the convenient store. Three cans of spam, beer and bread. This would be the dinner. Discussing the day, Mitch thought the fishing would be better to do for fun.

Tiziano agreed. Lots of work and nearly lost the entire catch. Tiziano thought what a great time, yet doing each day would not be profitable. Tiziano was nauseated from the boat ride with the rough water.

The next day, Tiziano woke up at the small studio apartment. D had gone to work. They both were working, one at the pizza parlor and Rose as a waitress. Tiziano's day would be the same. Go to find his cousin at his girlfriend's apartment. Hit a doobie and back to the water front to dive for fish and just hanging out. Ride some waves and look for girls. D was a nice person, yet Tiziano was young and full of energy each day.

Tiziano before leaving from his home on the mainland had a girlfriend. Her name was Sherry. Tiziano loved her, yet she was like a butterfly, even sleeping with Tiziano's so-called friend. He was happy he had left and ventured out on his own. This assisted him to forget about her.

Tiziano's sister had sent a post card prior to leaving Kauai. It stated that Sherry was coming to the island and would be staying in Waikiki.

Tiziano's sister Gina, stated she talked to Sherry, that she had inquired about Tiziano. Tiziano had Sherry's number on the mainland. He had been with Sherry for 2 years on and off. Tiziano had come to the conclusion she was good for one thing. Tiziano would follow up with Sherry.

The next week, Sherry arrived in Waikiki. Tiziano met her at the twin towers Hyatt Regency - beautiful hotel. Sherry was with another friend from the mainland. Tiziano did not have much to say.

He arrived at the hotel late one night. Slept with Sherry while her friend was on the queen bed next to them.

Tiziano had no respect for Sherry. She was from a broken family that had some money. Tiziano loved her or he thought. At this time, completed what he wanted, left in the morning without saying goodbye.

Sherry was not good for Tiziano. She was low life.

LOLLIPOP

The topless bar was just below the apartment complex. Tiziano and his cousin had not spent much time there. It cost money and neither had. All of Tiziano's money was coming from selling fish on the beach and or Puka Shells. Money was for food and few beers. Going out was few and far between.

D was always there for Tiziano and Mitch had so many girls after him. It was unfair, yet Mitch always came back with cash. He had food and or other items from his one-night stands.

Things were going well. Each day was full of fun in the sun.

One night, Mitch came home with some extra money. "Let's check the Lollipop tonight, Tiziano", Mitch suggested.

Tiziano was happy about that. It was not 5 minutes in the Bar Mitch had 2 girls. They were tourists buying him drinks. Tiziano was hanging out observing the nice ambience. So many beautiful Asian girls dancing.

"Let's go", Mitch stated. "These girls have a few doobies and want to walk on the beach, must been around 10 PM.

Down at the beach front, Mitch introduced this beautiful Blonde, 20 something, with long sandy colored hair to Tiziano.

Elsa was her name. Tiziano remembers nothing. Woke up on the beach the next morning. Mitch was gone. Elsa was gone.

Tiziano's eyes caught a glimpse of his cousin walking towards him. "Wow! Tiziano, you did not want to move last night. "How did it go with Elsa"? his cousin inquired. "Just fine, I guess. Yes, we smoked a few Js and then they had some whiskey". "That is what did it", Tiziano stated. I am not into that drink. It hurt me last night". "Yes, I could tell", Mitch replied.

"Hey! these girls want to go to breakfast. Come on we can shower at their apartment", stated Mitch.

"They are all sister from Florida", Four sisters and the mother. They have been here for 1 month". Mitch on another mission. Rollin each day … Tiziano thought.

Elsa was there smiling at Tiziano, "here hit this it will make you feel better". Post breakfast, Tiziano went down to the beach swimming. Mitch soon followed. "My gosh! this family is in love with me", Mitch stated to Tiziano.

Elsa gave me 40 dollars. Tiziano was lost for words. That would take 3 days to make that money when Tiziano was working. "Talk to you later, Tiziano, going for a stroll down the beach".

Tiziano was not complaining, however as Tiziano was laying there on a new beach towel that Mitch's girlfriend had bought him, up walked this big 30 something year old man and said, "are you with the one they call Mitch?"

Tiziano did not say anything. I am just here enjoying myself catching some rays. "I live there at the lollipop and my girlfriend's family live down the hall. Tell Mitch I want to talk". Tiziano was like, not again. He had already had enough trouble on Kauai.

Tiziano caught up with his cousin and explained about the big man they call, Ed. "Yes, ok", stated Mitch. "He is jealous that I did his girl. Yes, I was with all of them Tiziano", Mitch added. The first night post meeting them at the lollipop, we all went down to the pool side at the apartment.

"It was just like; they all wanted a part of me, even the mother", stated Mitch. "I guess she is around 40 yrs. old. I am not even worried about Ed", he added. It would not be pretty an 18 yr. That old man is embarrassing.

Tiziano was not into the trouble. He had encounter enough in Kauai, that day at Poipu. Tiziano could sense something was bothering Mitch. Even though he had so many girls each day and they were being very generous with him, he wasn't content.

Tiziano headed back to his small studio apartment. D and Rose were there. "What is going on, Tiziano? We have not seen you for 2 days". Tiziano explained he had been out with friends.

Tiziano was a bit exhausted with all the drama. Waikiki was moving too fast.

Two weeks ago, was working each day for Lelan Nishek at Kauai Nursery and Landscaping. Tiziano had left the job to follow his cousin. It seemed to be the wrong decision, however, Tiziano continued to enjoy his time away from the mainland. Tiziano gathered his thoughts.

The summer was near the end. October was next week. The tourists were still arriving; however, it was older folks. The everyday fun in the Hawaiian Sun was there, yet not the big spark that Tiziano had experienced 4 months ago. He could also feel his cousin just not this charismatic positive individual.

222

Tiziano's studio apartment was 322.

He had been there two months. Living on and off D and Rose were great. They always allowed Tiziano to stay, eat, shower and live there. It was so small, yet there was a nice air conditioner and Tiziano enjoyed the company.

At times, Tiziano did not have a key, yet the apartment was open. They had some friends down the hall, kept a key and all seemed to be safe in the small complex. The only issue was Big Ed, the boyfriend of one of the sisters from Florida. Ed did not like Mitch and he knew I was the cousin; therefore, he did not like me.

Tiziano for whatever reason had mistakenly gone to Ed s apartment a few times. Instead of 322, would take the elevator from the street to 222. Big Ed answered the door, "what the fuck are you doing here?", he yelled to Tiziano. I will waste you and your cousin. Tiziano attempted to explain, yet Big Ed was livid.

Tiziano ran down the stairs and out to the beach. Later when the sun was down, he caught up with Mitch. "Yes, I have done the same thing", explained Mitch. "You can get mixed up". The issue was Mitch was sleeping with Big Ed's girlfriend. Big Ed worked on another island and was gone for 1 week at a time sometimes 2 weeks. The Florida family was in love with Mitch. They had all had a taste of him. Tiziano partied with Elsa, yet never experienced the others. "Let's go!", Tiziano stated to His cousin, "come let's go to D and Roses place".

The night was hot, yet winter season had cooled down the day time hot Hawaiian sun. Rose and D were happy to see Tiziano. They were not so happy to see Mitch. He really never was there and Rose was his supposedly his Girlfriend, yet not ……

Mitch was King in Hawaii when it came to entertaining girls. Tiziano had observed him with at least 30 different females in 4 months. It did not seem fair, yet there was always money and food.

Mitch was doing his part for their little family during that graduation present from Tiziano's parents. The one week had turned into nearly half a year.…

Tiziano had just started to sleep post-enjoying.

"D, OPEN THE FUCKING DOOR!!"

My god it was Big Ed! Tiziano's heart started racing. It brought back memories of Brennecke's Beach, the day Tiziano almost lost his life twice in a matter of hours.

"Quiet, Mitch", stated to Tiziano. Rose, answer the door. Tell him we are not here". Rose did not open the door, yet looked out the peep hole. "A fucking gun", Rose whispered. You could hear Big Ed saying, "ya take a look and tell your boyfriend Mitch I am here in 222".

The next morning, Tiziano needed to reinvigorate himself. "Mitch", Tiziano stated, "I am thinking about looking for a different apartment". "What is your thought, Tiziano"? "I am thinking about calling Mr. Wizard".

"Haha", Mitch laughed. "Hey, Big Ed was drunk no need to be excited", he added. Tiziano had few dimes. The call was made back to the mainland. Tiziano's sister Gina answered the phone. She was very happy to hear from Tiziano. "We have been worried about you", she quipped.

Arriving back in the mainland, to that little village in the mountains felt like being on the red carpet at the academy Awards.

Tiziano was so thrilled to see his family. He had accomplished his goal of being on his own yet there was nothing like Home.

ORIGINAL PICTURE OF TIZIANO AND MITCH 1980